Lizard Sees the World

by SUSAN TEWS
Illustrated by GEORGE CRESPO

CLARION BOOKS/New York

With love to Bob,
who sees the world so well
—S.T.

To my beautiful daughter, Mercy
—G.C.

Clarion Books
a Houghton Mifflin Company imprint
215 Park Avenue South, New York, NY 10003
Text copyright © 1997 by Susan Tews
Illustrations copyright © 1997 by George Crespo

The illustrations for this book were executed in oil paint on vellum paper.
The text is set in 14/20-point Meridien.

For information about this and other Houghton Mifflin
trade and reference books and multimedia products,
visit The Bookstore at Houghton Mifflin on the World Wide Web
at (http://www.hmco.com/trade/).

Printed in the USA

Library of Congress Cataloging-in-Publication Data

Tews, Susan.
Lizard sees the world / by Susan Tews ; illustrated by George Crespo.
p.   cm.
Summary: Lizard finds his concept of the world challenged
when he goes out to find the edge of the world.
ISBN 0-395-72662-X
[1. Lizards—Fiction. 2. Animals—Fiction.
3. Travel—Fiction. 4. Curiosity—Fiction.] I. Crespo, George, ill. II. Title.
PZ7.T29647Li 1996
[Fic]—dc20   95-9640
CIP
AC

HOR 10 9 8 7 6 5 4 3 2 1

Lizard flicked his tail and rolled his eyes all around. He was getting ready to go on a journey. Other lizards only wanted to catch flies, but Lizard wanted to see the whole world.

Lizard was planning to climb to the place where the sky meets the earth. When he reached the topmost edge of the world, he would look down. He would see the whole world below him!

He wanted to tell the others all about it when he returned.

Lizard darted off on his journey. Along the way he stopped by the gurgling river, where Trout was swimming.

Trout said, "Good morning, Lizard. Are you going some-where?"

"Good morning, Trout," Lizard answered excitedly. "I'm going to see the world."

Trout said, "Ahh, the wet and bubbly world. It has powerful currents to take us wherever we want to swim. The world is a fine place, isn't it?"

And Trout swam off happily.

Lizard wanted to tell her that the world was a *bowl*. He would have told her that the river running along the bottom of the bowl was just one of many things in the world. But Trout was gone.

Lizard's tail splashed in the river. "When I come back, I'll tell Trout all about the world," he thought as he went on his way.

Lizard came upon Jackrabbit scampering out of the underbrush.

"Good morning, Jackrabbit," said Lizard. "I am going all the way to where the earth meets the sky." Lizard held his head high.

"Why?" Jackrabbit asked.

"So I can see the whole world," Lizard said. "When I come back, I'll tell you all about it."

Jackrabbit scratched behind his ear. "I can tell you about the world, Lizard," he said. "The world is all green, leafy things. The world grows delicious things to eat and makes a comfortable place for my little hares. Look here."

Lizard stuck his head between the willow branches and peered into Jackrabbit's grassy home. Pairs of tiny eyes shone back.

Lizard knew that green, leafy things were only a part of the world. He began to tell Jackrabbit that the world was a bowl, but when he looked up Jackrabbit was gone, off to nibble some grasses.

Lizard flexed his legs. Then he ran along, farther and farther.

Soon Lizard reached the steep cliff wall. He hooked his toes into the crevices. He climbed and climbed.

He came upon Hummingbird hovering among the flowers. Hummingbird asked, "Where are you going, Lizard?"

Lizard said, "I'm on my way to the top of the world."

"Enjoy the warm winds, then," said Hummingbird. "They rise to the top of the world. Breezes and gusts, that's the world—and a bit of nectar, too."

Lizard knew that the winds were only one part of the world. He wanted very much to tell Hummingbird this, but in a wink Hummingbird was gone, off to the next patch of flowers.

16

Lizard gulped the brisk air and climbed higher.

Snake was sunning herself on a slab of rock as Lizard passed by.

Snake said, "Lizard, where are you going?"

"I am on a journey to the top of the world," said Lizard.

"Such a long journey," said Snake. "What will you do when you get there?"

Lizard said, "I will look down and see the whole world."

"You'll see rocks," said Snake. "Rocks everywhere. Warm on top, cool underneath—nice rocks, but rocks all the same."

Snake slithered away. She was gone before Lizard could tell her there was much more to the world than rocks.

Tired and hot, Lizard stretched out beneath Snake's shady rock. Soon he felt refreshed, and he continued on his way.

Lizard climbed higher now. As he clung to the cliff, he looked at the mighty walls all around him. The cliffs with their crags and hollows rose to the sky.

He thought, "What a view I'll have when I reach the top! At last I will see the whole world! When I return and tell the other animals about it, they'll be amazed!"

Lizard pressed on, higher and higher.

As he neared the very top, Lizard didn't think he could climb another step. When he looked up, he saw Eagle soaring high above him.

Eagle called down, "Where are you going, Lizard?"

"I am going to the top of the world," Lizard called back. "Tell me, from where you are flying, can you see the whole bowl that is the world?"

Eagle just laughed and soared away.

Wondering why Eagle had laughed, Lizard climbed closer and closer to the rim. He pulled himself higher and higher.

At last he poked his head above the top of the cliff.
Lizard looked out beyond the rocky rim, and he saw . . .

. . . that the world did not end at the cliff's edge. It only began there! The world went on in every direction for as far as he could see.

Now Lizard understood why Eagle had laughed.

The bowl where Lizard lived was only a canyon sunk into the wide plain all around him. His canyon was a magnificent bowl, to be sure—but it was only part of the whole world.

Then Lizard laughed too. His idea of the world had been as foolish as Trout's, or Jackrabbit's, or Hummingbird's, or Snake's.

Someday he'd go back and tell them so.

But not yet. . . .

The sun cast a golden light on everything that lay before him.
There was so much of the world to see!
Lizard flicked his tail and rolled his eyes all around.
And then Lizard darted off to see the rest of the world.

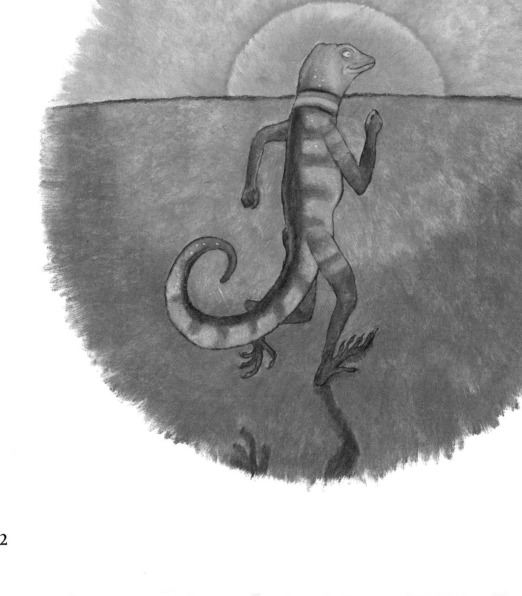